THE STORY OF THE

# Falling Star

WESTERN REGIONAL ABORIGINAL LAND COUNCIL

THE STORY OF THE

# Falling Star

TOLD BY ELSIE JONES
WITH DRAWINGS BY DOUG JONES
AND COLLAGES BY KARIN DONALDSON

ABORIGINAL STUDIES PRESS · CANBERRA 1989

*THE AUSTRALIAN INSTITUTE OF ABORIGINAL AND TORRES STRAIT ISLANDER STUDIES* is grateful for the generous assistance of the Department of Aboriginal Affairs in the publication of this book.

*FIRST PUBLISHED IN 1989, REPRINTED 1991 BY*
Aboriginal Studies Press
for the Australian Institute of Aboriginal and Torres Strait Islander Studies
GPO Box 553, Canberra, ACT 2601.

The views expressed in this publication are those of the authors and not necessarily those of the Australian Institute of Aboriginal and Torres Strait Islander Studies.

*NATIONAL LIBRARY OF AUSTRALIA CATALOGUING-IN-PUBLICATION DATA:*

Jones, Elsie 1917–   .
   The story of the falling star.

   ISBN 0 85575 199 1.

   (1). Aborigines, Australian—Legends—Juvenile literature. (2). Aborigines, Australian—Folklore— Juvenile literature. I. Jones, Doug, 1962–   . II. Donaldson, Karin, 1943–   . III. Australian Institute of Aboriginal and Torres Strait Islander Studies. IV. Title.
398.2'6'0994

*SPONSORED BY THE* Western Regional Aboriginal Land Council.

*TRANSCRIBED AND LAYOUT BY* Karin Donaldson.

*PHOTOGRAPHY BY* Karin Donaldson and Anthony Pease.

*DECORATED MAPS BY* Murray Butcher.

*DRAWINGS BY* Doug Jones.

*DESIGN OF COVER FRONTS AND BACKS BY* Maureen MacKenzie, Aboriginal Studies Press.

*ADDITIONAL TYPESETTING IN* Compugraphic Lubalin Graph by Aboriginal Studies Press.

*PRINTED IN* Australia by Griffin Press, Netley, SA.

5000 08 91

JIM WHYMAN

KARINA SLOANE

HILDA BARLOW

SELINA HALL

MERVYN WILLIAMS

THIS BOOK IS DEDICATED TO THE MEMORY OF FIVE MUCH-LOVED MEMBERS OF OUR PEOPLE WHO HELPED WITH THE MAKING OF THE BOOK BUT DID NOT LIVE TO SEE IT FINISHED

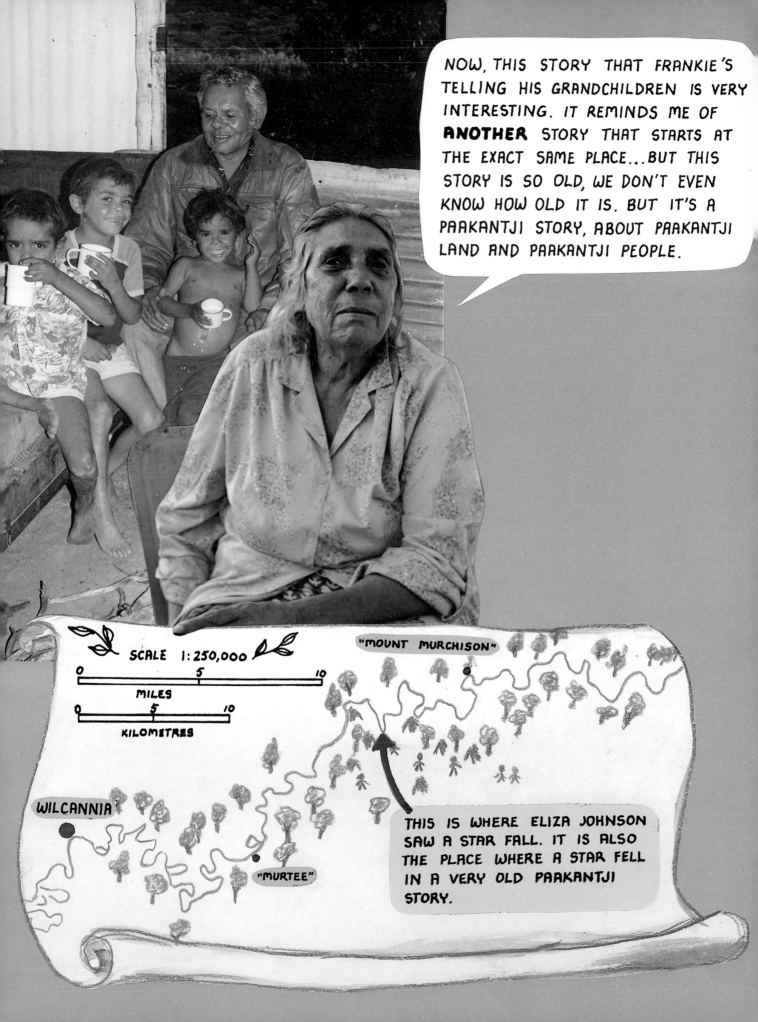

I HEARD THIS STORY FROM MY GRANNY, SARAH CABBAGE AND I HEARD OTHER OLD PAAKANTJI PEOPLE TELL THIS STORY TOO... AND **THEY** WOULD'VE HEARD IT TOLD BY THE OLD PEOPLE IN THE PAAKANTJI CAMPS WHEN **THEY** WERE YOUNG.

MALKARRA WOULD DO A LOT OF BAD THINGS...
STEAL, SNEAK AROUND AND LIVE IN CAVES
BY HIMSELF. HE'D STEAL WOMEN AND KILL
YOU...A MURDERER OR CRIMINAL. YOU
NEVER FELT LIKE YOU COULD **TRUST** HIM.

IN SOME WAYS IT SEEMED LIKE MALKARRA
WAS TRYING TO **DESTROY** THINGS.

HE TOLD THEM THERE WAS GOING TO BE SOMETHING VERY DANGEROUS HAPPENING, ONE DAY VERY SOON. AND HE TOLD THEM THEY ALL HAD TO BE PREPARED AND READY FOR THIS.

A GROUP OF PEOPLE SAID TO GO AND GET PUNRITJ, AND GET HIM TO HEAR THIS STORY. BECAUSE THEY WEREN'T SURE OF MALKARRA.

PARRI YAAMARI THALTILA YIKI WIIMPATJA KULPAAN THURLAKA PARLKU!

MINHA PARLKU WATHU?

"COME AND HEAR THE BAD NEWS THIS BLACKFELLA'S TELLING US!"
"WHAT'S HE SAYING?"

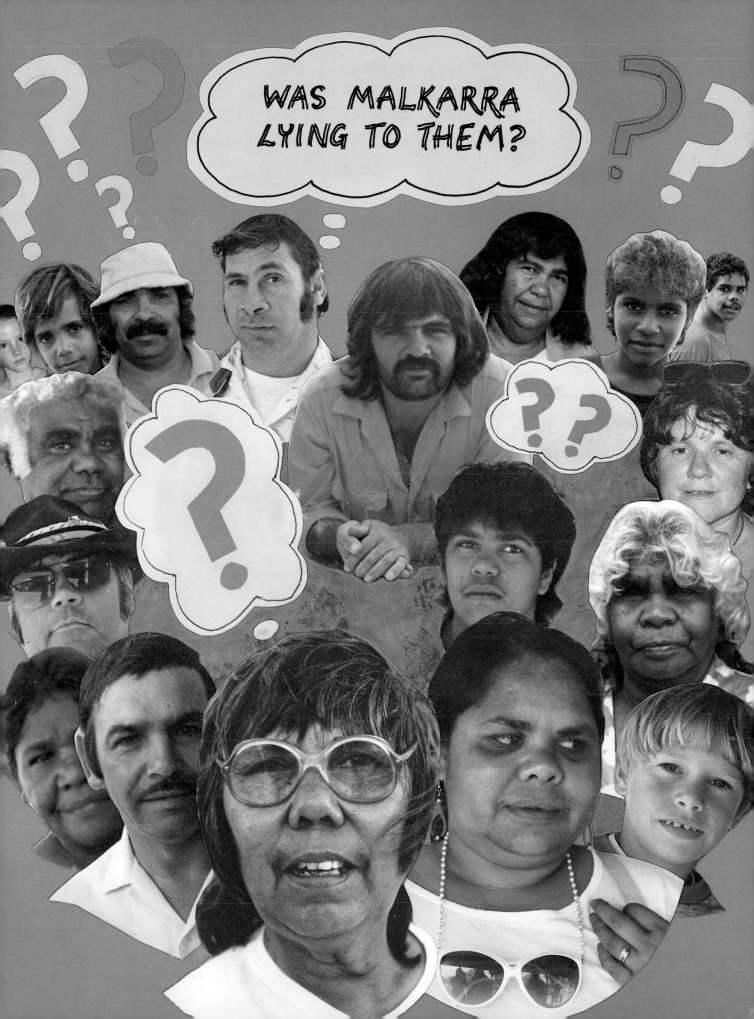

MALKARRA WAS TELLING THE **TRUTH**. HE **KNEW** WHAT WAS HAPPENING. BUT MOST PEOPLE WOULDN'T BELIEVE HIM BECAUSE HE BROKE A LOT OF THE LAWS THEY HAD.

MALKARRA KNEW THERE WAS DANGER. HE COULD FEEL AND SEE THINGS IN HIS MIND THAT WAS GOING TO HAPPEN. AND HE SAID TO FOLLOW THE WAY HE WENT.

IN THE END, PUNRITJ TOLD THEM IT WAS TRUE WHAT MALKARRA WAS SAYING, AND THEN THEY **DID** BELIEVE PUNRITJ.

GRANNY AND AUNTIE ADA TOLD US THAT AT THE FINISH THEY COULD SEE THAT MALKARRA WAS TELLING THEM THE TRUTH... BUT IT WAS A BIT **LATE**... AND A LOT OF THEM GOT **CAUGHT**.

HOW DID THEY GET CAUGHT?

YEARS AGO, WHEN WE CAME OUT HERE, THERE WAS SOME DIFFERENT COLOURED STONE AS WELL AS WHAT YOU SEE NOW. THERE WAS A LOT OF **BLACK** STONE HERE...THAT SORT OF DULL BLACK LIKE YOU SEE IN OUR PEOPLE'S OLD FIREPLACES. AND IT HAD **SHINY** BITS LIKE BLACK MARBLE, TOO, AND BITS OF **GREEN**, AND BITS THAT WERE **WHITE-ISH** LIKE THE FAT IN A SHEEP. I FOUND A BIT OF THAT WHITE STONE SOMEWHERE ELSE TO SHOW YOU WHAT USED TO BE HERE.

THEN IT STARTED TO RAIN, LIKE MALKARRA SAID IT WOULD...

YITHU MAKARRA THUTHATHU NHANTAMA PALJARTA!

"THIS RAIN JUST KEEPS ON POURING!"

WHEN THEY GOT HERE TO MOUNT GRENFELL, THEY HAD TO TAKE THE INJURED ONES UP TO THE TOP OF THE HILLS. THERE ARE SOME CAVES THEY COULD SHELTER IN, AND THEY WERE UP THERE FOR DAYS AND DAYS. THEY COULDN'T **DO** ANYTHING, BECAUSE THE WATER WAS ALL AROUND THE SIDES OF THE HILL.

AFTER THE RAIN HAD EASED OFF, THERE WAS STILL A LOT OF WATER AROUND. BUT SOME OF THEM GOT DOWN TO SEE WHAT HAD HAPPENED. AND THERE WERE SOME PEOPLE **STILL** ARRIVING, COMING UP THE HILL.

AFTER THE WATER STARTED GOING DOWN, THE PEOPLE MOVED ON. BUT BEFORE THEY WENT, THEY HAD TO LEAVE STORIES ON THE ROCK FOR ANY OTHER PEOPLE THAT WAS COMING BEHIND THEM, LOOKING FOR THEM. AND YOU SEE THE PICTURES ON THESE STONES? YOU'LL SEE **KANGAROOS AND EMUS**! THAT MEANS "THE KANGAROO AND EMU PEOPLE BEEN HERE." KANGAROO IS ONE OF THE TOTEMS ON THE **MAKWARRA** SIDE. EMU ARE ON THE **KIILPARRA** SIDE. THAT'S PAAKANTJI LANGUAGE. THAT WAS THEIR RELIGION. WE CALL IT OUR **TOTEM** OR OUR **MEAT**.

SO MY **DAUGHTERS' CHILDREN** AND MY **SISTERS' DAUGHTERS' CHILDREN** ARE EMU TOO. BUT MY **SON'S** DAUGHTER GETS HER MEAT THROUGH **HER MOTHER'S** SIDE. MY GRANNY EXPLAINED THE STRICT RULES AND LAWS TO ME...SHE COULDN'T **EAT** EMU BECAUSE HER MEAT WAS EMU, AND SHE COULDN'T **MARRY** ANYONE WHO WAS EMU OR ANY OF THE OTHER MEATS ON THE KIILPARRA SIDE.

AND YOU WERE SAYING THAT THERE ARE PRINTS IN THE ROCK HERE, LIKE AT MOUNT GRENFELL, AUNTIE ELSIE?

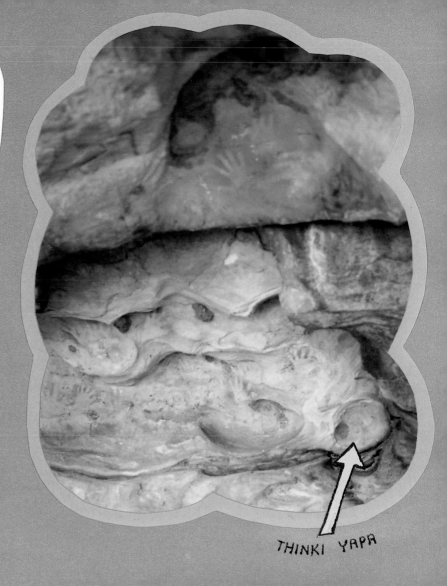

THINKI YAPA

YES! ONE TIME I WAS OUT HERE WITH OLD NGARLU LUCY AND HER DAUGHTER CLARA. GRANNY KATE BUGMY WAS HERE TOO. AND THESE OLD LADIES WERE TELLING US HOW THE ROCK WAS SOFT WHEN THESE PEOPLE CLIMBED UP TO SHELTER HERE. THEY LEFT **KNEE MARKS...THINKI YAPA**. THERE'S MORE THAN ONE CAVE WITH KNEE MARKS. AND THERE'S **ELBOW MARKS...KUPU YAPA**; AND THERE'S **FOOT** AND **HAND PRINTS...THINA YAPA** AND **MARA YAPA**. THE FOOT PRINTS ARE WELL UP ON TOP OF THE RANGES WHERE THE FLAT ROCKS ARE.

PLACES THE PAAKANTJI WIIMPATJA WALKED TO IN THIS STORY

PURLI NGAANGKALITJI

TILPA IS HERE TODAY

PAAKA: DARLING RIVER

FLOOD

PAAKA

ACRES BILLABONG

"MOUNT MURCHISON"

MUTAWINTJI

WILCANNIA IS HERE TODAY

"MURTEE"

MOUNT GRENF

BROKEN HILL IS HERE TODAY

THE NINE MILE

"MULCHARA PARK"

"BILLILLA"

"WEINTERIGA"

CHRISTMAS ROCKS

CORINYA HILLS

MENINDEE IS HERE TODAY

TALYAWALKA

MOUNT MANARA

IVANHOE IS HERE TODAY

"HARCOURT"

TARTNA POINT

FLOOD

PAAKA: DARLING RIVER

POONCARIE IS HERE TODAY

LAKE VICTORIA

WENTWORTH IS HERE TODAY

MURRAY RIVER

SCALE

0    25    50    75    100

KILOMETRES

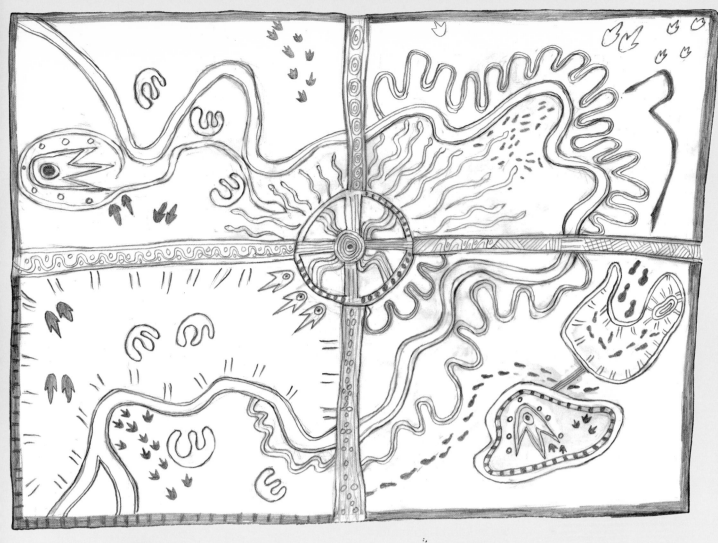

 spirit of Malkarra

 camps

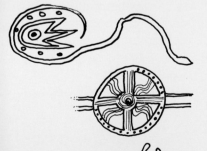 Malkarra warning the people that something bad is going to happen

the star falling

explosion, danger

floods

 people's footprints showing their travels

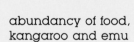 river

abundancy of food, kangaroo and emu

 food is scarce

hills

 Nine Mile Hill, the place where Malkarra was last seen

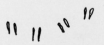 celebrations by those who survived death

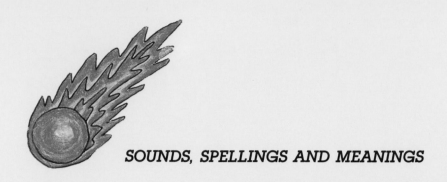

## SOUNDS, SPELLINGS AND MEANINGS

The Paakantji language is special enough to need its own way of spelling. The spelling system used in this book will help those who do not speak any Paakantji and those who speak Paakantji but are not used to seeing it written down. We have selected one letter (or two letters together) to always stand for the same sound. Paakantji has twenty-six sounds that are different enough to give different meanings. In English **pill** and **bill** have different meanings because **p** and **b** are different sounds. In Paakantji **p** and **b** do not give different sounds or meanings. The same applies to **k** and **g**, and to **t** and **d**. In this book we have chosen to spell the name of the language as 'Paakantji', but it could be written as 'Baakantji', 'Baagandji' or other variations. The word still sounds and means the same. In Paakantji there are four different types of **n** and **l** sounds which give different meanings, so these must be written differently.

These are the sounds in Paakantji.

| | |
|---|---|
| a | like in English b**u**t |
| i | like in English f**i**ll |
| u | like in English p**u**ll |
| aa | like in English f**a**ther |
| ii | like in English mach**i**ne |
| uu | close to English p**oo**l |
| k | between English **k** or **g** |
| l | as in English |
| m | as in English |
| n | as in English |
| ng | like in English si**ng**er, not fi**ng**er |
| p | between English **p** or **b** |
| r | similar to English but tip of tongue curled back |
| rl, rn, rt | made with tip of tongue curled back to touch roof of mouth |
| rr | like Italian or Scottish **r**, but quicker, made by flapping tip of tongue on ridge behind teeth |
| t | between English **t** or **d** |
| th, nh, lh | made with tip of tongue between teeth and blade of tongue on rear of top teeth |
| tj, nj, lj | made with blade of tongue behind top teeth and tip of tongue behind bottom teeth |
| w | as in English, may be silent before **u** |
| y | as in English, may be silent before **i** |

Here is how you sound out some of the words in the story.

| | |
|---|---|
| Malkarra | mal (**mul**berry) ka (**cu**t) rra (**ru**n) |
| Punritj | pun (**bu**ll + **n**) ritj (**ri**ch) |
| purli yithu ngaangkalaana (the star is falling) | pu (**bu**ll) rli (**li**ck)  yi (**i**n) thu (**do**)  ngaang (si**ng** + **are** + si**ng**) ka (**gu**t) laa (**lar**ge) na (**nu**t) |

An important rule in Paakantji is that the stress falls on the first syllable in every word. The following is a list of some of the key words used in this story giving their meanings, but note that words can end in different ways depending on the role they play in each sentence. Verbs, for example, often have different extensions to show tense and person.

| | |
|---|---|
| kapa- | to follow |
| kaaka- | to call out |
| kiilparra, makwarra | two 'sides' of religion |
| kulpa- | to tell, to talk |
| kumpatja | big |
| kupu | elbow |
| makarra | rain |
| Malkarra | bad Clever Person in this story |
| mara | hand |
| marima- | to help, to look after |
| marri | really, very much |
| minha | what |
| miikika | doctor, Clever Person, spiritual advisor |
| murrarta | quick |
| ngampu- | to rumble |
| ngamuru | big, black river goanna |
| ngapa, nga- | I, me, my etc |
| ngaangka- | to fall |
| ngina | us |
| ngiyi | yes |
| nhantama | again |
| nhiki | coals of fire |
| palpa | ashes |
| paljarta | wait |
| parlku | word, speech |
| parna | broadly striped river goanna |
| papu- | to come out |
| parri- | to go, to walk, to come |
| Paakantji | Aboriginal people and language of the Darling River |
| purli | star |
| Punritj | good Clever Person in this story |
| puungka | shelter, dwelling |
| thalti- | to hear, to listen |
| thina | foot |
| thinki | knee |
| thingka- | to get up |
| thurlaka | bad |
| thutha- | to pour (rain) |
| waljpunja | stubborn |
| watharna | way over there |
| wathu | that one |
| waankawaankaathu | 'a rogue', one who is bribing or coaxing |
| wiimpatja | Aboriginal person |
| yapa | track |
| yaparra | camp |
| yaamari | here |
| yilayi | hey! |
| yithi-, yithu-, yiki- | this, these, etc |

## ACKNOWLEDGEMENTS

THE WESTERN REGIONAL ABORIGINAL LAND COUNCIL which sponsored the production of this book, would like to thank everyone who has participated. There have been many tasks involved, and many people have enthusiastically offered their time and talents to the project. We are proud of the generous teamwork that has made this book possible, for without the contribution of this very large number of people, it would have remained a dream. Together we have produced a book that celebrates Paakantji land and heritage. Special thanks are due to the following people, organisations and groups.

Brenda Riley, Trish Charnley, the late Hilda Barlow, Suzanne Hall, Badger Bates and Sarah Martin who organised transport and tucker and/or helped with children's activities on trips to the Star Site (Purli Ngaangkalitji), Mount Grenfell and Mount Manara. We also thank the group of ten year old Wilcannia kids who did a great job building the old-style Paakantji camp for the scene at the Star Site.

Thanks to all those who worked so hard and efficiently to organise the community barbecue: Lionel Dutton, Colleen Harris, Gloria Quayle, Steven Harris, Rhonda Riley, Christine Smith, Margie Ann Whyman, Phyllis Whyman, Edie Williams, Joyce Williams, Kerry King, Patricia Whyman and Aileen Harris; and Dennis Williams and Denis Dunlop who provided the meat. Many thanks also to: Kerry King and Abigail Hall who helped Doug Jones paint up the kids; the kids who were so enthusiastic about participating in it; and all the people who came on trips, joined in at the barbecue and who appear in photographs throughout the book.

We thank the Principals and staff of Wilcannia's schools—The Central School, St Therese's School and Muurrpa Puungka Pre-School—who showed great interest in the project and allowed the children to take part in trips and activities as part of their school work.

Special thanks are due to: Frank Johnson for relating the family story that begins the book; to fourteen year old Murray Butcher who did the decorated maps; to Peter Thompson for help with writing down the Paakantji and the notes on pronunciation, editorial advice, negotiation with the publisher, helping with fund-raising and constant encouragement; and to the Aboriginal people of Wilcannia who voted on the title for the book, with special thanks to Margie Ann Whyman whose suggestion for the title won the final vote.

Aboriginal people of the region made helpful comments on the book and the layout was developed in response to the community's preferences in book design. Other people experienced in education, publishing or layout provided useful suggestions on the format of the book including: Gloria King, Sylvia Hale, Maureen MacKenzie, Jennifer Raines, Jo Black, Gai Smith, Joanne Spiller, Bernard Spiller and the late Mervyn Williams. Special thanks to Anthony Pease, who made many valuable contributions to the layout and who assisted with photography. His experience and ideas in both these areas were a great help.

For permission to use their photographs, we thank: Sarah Martin for the ones of Mount Manara Caves on pages 71 and 75; Billie Paul for those of the late Mervyn Williams; Chris Donaldson for one of the photos on page 50; Bob Wilson for the photo on page 12; the Mitchell Library for the historic photographs on pages 12, 20, 22 and 80; and the National Library of Australia in Canberra for the one on page 26. We also thank Norm Evans of 'Quick as a Flash' (Doncaster, Victoria), who offered advice and took great care with the accuracy of the colours in our photographs; and Bob Cooper of the Australian National University for his photograph of the Southern Cross region of the night sky which we used on our endpapers.

We thank the following individuals who worked hard to secure financial backing: William Bates, Graham Carter, Barbara Flick, Ron Plunkett, Maureen O'Donnell, Gabrielle Jennings, Nora McManus, Brian Murnane and Joan Hamilton.

The following bodies have helped with funding during the eight years it has taken to develop this book: Aboriginal Arts Board, Australian Institute of Aboriginal Studies, Benedictine Sisters, Blessed Sacrament Fathers (Melbourne), Brigidine Sisters (New South Wales), Christian Brothers (Strathfield), Daughters of Charity (Eastwood), De la Salle Brothers (Kensington), Divine Word Missionaries (Epping), Dominican Sisters (New South Wales), Faithful Companions of Jesus, Good Samaritan Sisters (Mount Magnet), Knights of the Southern Cross (Chelsea), Little Company of Mary (Kogarah), Loretto Sisters (Albert Park), Marist Brothers (Southern Province), Marist Fathers (Sydney), Missionary Priests of the Sacred Heart, Missionary Sisters of Service (Parkes), Missionary Sisters of the Society of Mary, Presentation Sisters (Melbourne and Wagga), Salesian Fathers, Scalabrinian Fathers, St John of God Brothers (Burwood), St Vincent de Paul Society (Broken Hill Conference and New South Wales), Sisters of Mercy (Bathurst, Goulburn, Gunnedah, Melbourne and Singleton), Sisters of Charity (Potts Point), Sisters of St Joseph (Lochinvar, North Goulburn and Perthville).

WESTERN REGIONAL ABORIGINAL LAND COUNCIL
Broken Hill, February 1989

# PEOPLE WHO APPEAR IN THE STORY

Hilda Barlow
Angela Bates
Badger Bates
Bilyara Bates
Chantel Bates
Diane 'Dicey' Bates
Fiona Bates
Jim Bates
Kayleen Bates
Valda Bates
William Bates
Peter Boon
Jeremy Briar-Falla
Lenny Briar
Tibby Briar
Alice Bugmy
Ashlee Bugmy
Benjy Bugmy
Catherine Bugmy
Chelsea Bugmy
Heidi Bugmy
Louise Bugmy
Marissa Bugmy
Murray Butcher
Ben Charnley
Rowena Charnley
Damien Clark
Amy Donaldson
Frances Donaldson
Sarah Donaldson
Stacey Lee Dunlop
Lionel Dutton
Twila Dutton
Gloria Ebsworth
Leah Ebsworth
Mandy Ebsworth
Ethel Edwards
Angela Green
Robert Green
Abigail Hall

Dennis Hall
Doug Hall
Selina Hall
Suzanne Hall
Abry Harris
Aileen Harris
Alf 'Tossle' Harris
Andrew 'Blacks' Harris
Casey Harris
Colleen Harris
Dwayne Harris
Jason Harris
Les 'Waddy' Harris
Marilyn Harris
Marsha Harris
Mervyn Harris
Steven Harris
Steven 'Monkey' Harris
Tania Harris
Christine 'Nhuni' Hunter
Diane Hunter
Jeffrey Hunter
Bradley Johnson
Raymond Hunter
Cecil Johnson
Clint Johnson
Frank Johnson
Kevin Johnson
Rene Johnson
Brendan Jones
Doreen Jones
Doug Jones
Douglas Jones
Elsie Jones
Joshua Jones
Leetisha Jones
Nelson Jones
Teegan Jones
Cassidy Kennedy
Melissa Kennedy

Molly Kennedy
Christopher 'ET' Kerwin
Derek Kerwin
Jessie Kerwin
Joan Kerwin
Kayleen Kerwin
Phillip Kerwin
Robbie Kerwin
Samantha 'Saami'
   Kerwin
Gloria King
Kerry King
Linda King
Tammy King
Eileen Kirby
Jimmy Kirby
'Brownie' Lawson
Dennis Lawson
Jeremy Lawson
Gerard Martin
John Martin
Sarah Martin
Doreen Mitchell
Erica Mitchell
Ernie Mitchell
Irene Mitchell
John Mitchell
Johnno Mitchell
Junette Mitchell
David Newitt
Kellie Newitt
Michael O'Connor
Amy Quayle
John A Quayle
Timothy Quayle
Brenda Riley
Rhonda Riley
Karen Sloane
Karina Sloane
Kim Sloane

Justin Sloane
Natasha Sloane
Christine Smith
Kelly Smith
Kylie Smith
Noel Smith
Shannon Smith
Leslie Sullivan
Mervyn Sullivan
Warlpa Thompson
Balaram Thorburn
Gopal Thorburn
Krishna Thorburn
Amanda Whitton
Kerry-Ann Whitton
Phillip Whitton
Gladys Whyman
Jim Whyman
Johnothon Whyman
Lenny 'Black Boy'
   Whyman
Margie Ann Whyman
Michael Whyman
Owen Whyman
Patricia Whyman
Phyllis Whyman
Alison Williams
Barney Williams
Edie 'Edie Girl' Williams
Fred Williams
Joyce Williams
Kenneth Williams
Kevin 'Blacks' Williams
Lottie Williams
Mervyn 'Crow' Williams
Samantha Williams
Sandra Williams
Lionel Troy Wilson
David Young
Robert Young